Locked Out

Story by Leonie Bennett
Pictures by Arlene Adams

OXFORD

Suzie ran out of school. Gran was waiting. Boxer and the babies were waiting, too.

"Come on, Gran," said Suzie. "Let's go home."

Gran pushed the buggy and Suzie walked the dog.

When they got home, the babies were asleep. Gran looked for her key.

She looked in one pocket. Then she looked in the other pocket. "Where is my key?" she said.

She looked in the first pocket again.
"Where is it?" she said.

"Let me help," said Suzie. And she looked in Gran's pockets, too... but there was no key.

“What can we do?” said Gran. “We are locked out.”

"Let's try the back door," said Suzie.
But the back door was locked.

“Let’s try the windows,” said Gran.
But the windows were locked, too.

"Oh dear," said Gran. "What are we going to do?"

Then the babies woke up. They were hungry and they were still tired. Soon they were crying.

Suzie was tired too. She gave Boxer a hug.

"Oh Boxer," she said. "Can you help us? You are a clever dog. Please, tell us what to do."

Gran laughed. “Boxer can’t help us,” she said. “He is not that clever.”

Suzie let Boxer go. The dog went to the back door and he pushed at the dog flap.

"Boxer is lucky," said Gran. "He can get into the house."

Suddenly Suzie said, "I can get into the house too!"

"I can get through the dog flap," she said.

Suzie pushed and
Gran helped.
The babies cried and
the dog barked and
Suzie went through
the dog flap.

Suzie was home at last!

She opened the door and in came Gran and the babies.

Gran gave Suzie a big hug.
“Thank you,” she said. “You are a very clever girl.”

Gran gave Boxer a biscuit.
"Thank you, too, Boxer," she said. "You are a very clever dog!"